SUPER SPECIAL #2
CHRISTMAS IN
COOPERSTOWN

Ballpark Mysteries®

Also by David A. Kelly

The MVP Series

Babe Ruth and the Baseball Curse

SUPER SPECIAL #2
CHRISTMAS IN
COOPERSTOWN

by David A. Kelly

illustrated by Mark Meyers

A STEPPING STONE BOOK™
Random House 🏠 New York

This book is dedicated to Major League Baseball, the National Baseball Hall of Fame, and all the great people of Cooperstown, New York. You all help to make baseball a home run for kids! —D.A.K.

Dad, thank you for all of the hours spent playing catch! —M.M.

"Cooperstown is the greatest place on Earth." —Hall of Fame pitcher Bob Feller

Text copyright © 2017 by David A. Kelly
Cover art and interior illustrations copyright © 2017 by Mark Meyers

Visit us on the Web!
SteppingStonesBooks.com
randomhousekids.com

Educators and librarians, for a variety of teaching tools, visit us at RHTeachersLibrarians.com

Library of Congress Cataloging-in-Publication Data is available upon request.
ISBN 978-0-399-55192-5 (trade) — ISBN 978-0-399-55193-2 (lib. bdg.) —
ISBN 978-0-399-55194-9 (ebook)

Printed in the United States of America
10 9 8 7 6 5 4 3 2 1

This book has been officially leveled by using the F&P Text Level Gradient™ Leveling System.

Contents

A Home Run Sleepover

It was Saturday morning, and Mike Walsh and his cousin Kate Hopkins bounded up the steps to the National Baseball Hall of Fame. As the door closed behind them, Mike saw a security guard place something behind a big cardboard box wrapped like a Christmas present.

Mike grabbed Kate's arm. "Hey!" he said as the guard ducked around the corner. "Did you see that? I'll bet that guard just stole a signed ball or something and hid it behind that present!"

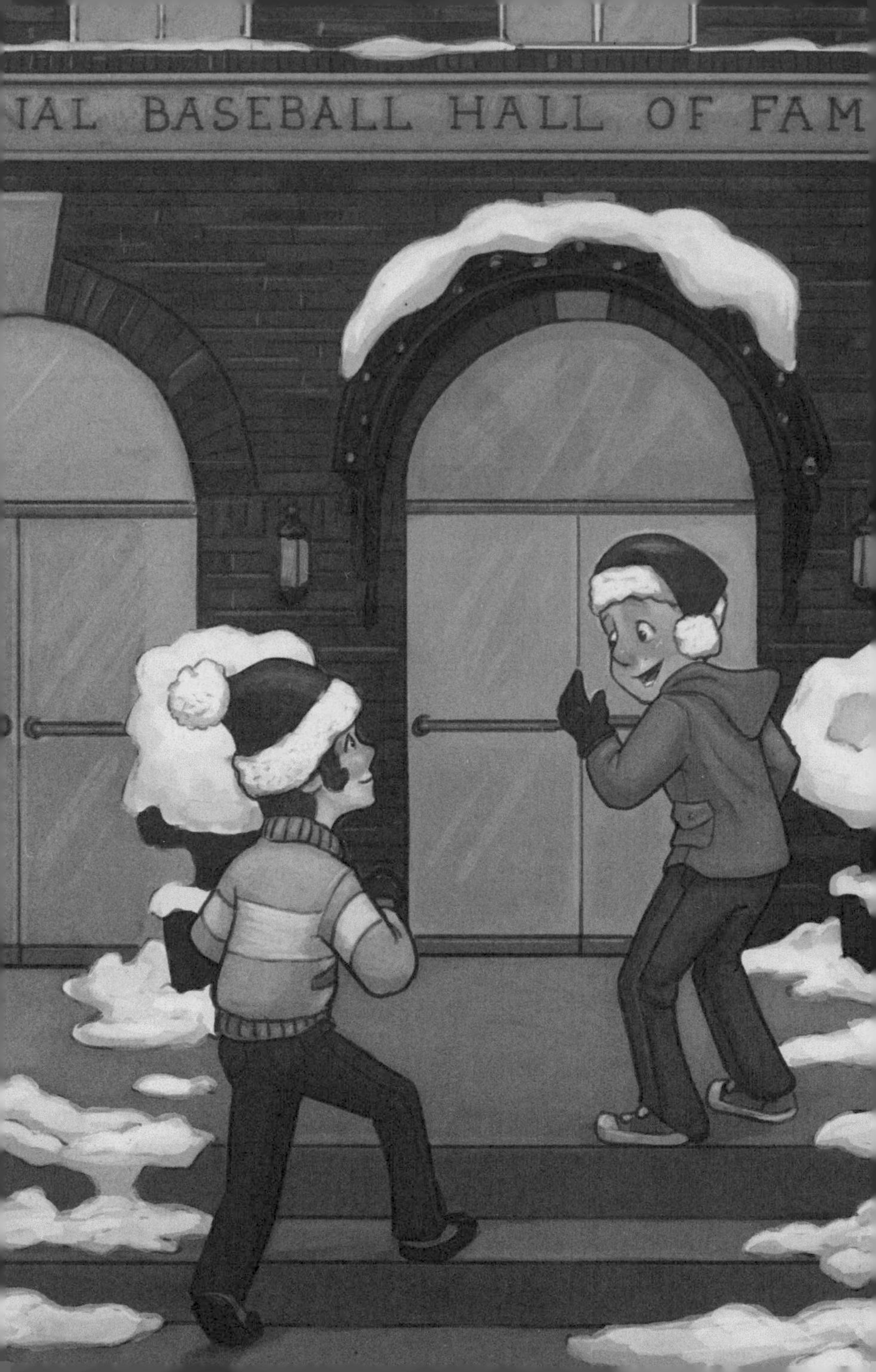
IAL BASEBALL HALL OF FAM

Kate sighed. Mike had a big imagination. "Come on!" she said. Kate walked over to the present. She reached down and lifted up a half-full water bottle.

"You're right!" she said. "It's Babe Ruth's famous water bottle that he used in game three of the 1932 World Series!"

Mike smiled weakly and blushed a little. "Okay, so I guess the guard was just thirsty," he said. "But the stuff in the Hall of Fame is worth millions! It's amazing that no one tries to steal it."

"That's why they have security guards!" Kate said. "You've been reading too many mystery stories."

Mike and Kate pulled off their red-and-white Santa hats and stamped the snow from their boots. It was December holiday break, and Mike and Kate were at the National

Baseball Hall of Fame in Cooperstown, New York, to help wrap presents for needy families. They both lived in town. Mike's parents owned a sporting goods store just up the street from the Hall of Fame. Kate's mom worked as a sports reporter.

Mike and Kate had joined a club called Cooperstown Cares with their friends. The club helped organize food drives, clothing drives, and toy drives. After spending the day wrapping presents at the Hall of Fame, the club was going to sleep over at Kate's house that night.

"Hey, you're here!" said a redheaded boy near the gift shop. It was Mike and Kate's friend Caleb from the Cooperstown Cares club. He waved them over. "Follow me. Everyone is in the research library in back. We're just getting started."

Ella, the woman at the ticket booth, waved

them in. She was wearing a bright green sweater with reindeer on the front. Mike and Kate ran after Caleb. They went past the museum's gift shop and into the Hall of Fame gallery. The gallery was filled with big bronze panels that listed the accomplishments of each baseball player who had been elected to the Hall of Fame. On the upper floors of the building was a museum filled with important baseball artifacts.

In the middle of the gallery stood a big Christmas tree decorated with all types of baseball ornaments. Caleb led them through the gallery to the research library. Sophia, Noah, Scott, and Logan, Mike and Kate's friends from school, were sitting at a long table wrapping a big pile of presents. Grace, a tall woman wearing a necklace made of tiny red-and-green lights, stood behind the table.

"There you two are!" Grace said. "Dig in. We have a lot of presents to wrap for the toy drive!"

Grace was a volunteer at the Hall of Fame. She ran the annual toy drive. She was also in charge of raising money to help build a new community center for Cooperstown. The town needed a bigger place where kids Mike and Kate's age could go after school and where families could get help with food, clothing, or whatever else they needed. The Cooperstown Cares club was helping with the toy drive.

Mike and Kate grabbed presents from the big pile at the end of the table and started wrapping. Grace had all different kinds of paper, ribbons, and bows laid out on the table. Every few minutes, one of the kids would carry a big stack of wrapped gifts out to the tree in the gallery. In between, everyone dipped into a bowl of candy canes in the middle of the table. As they wrapped presents, they twirled the candy canes around in their mouths.

Just before lunchtime, Grace went into the office she shared with Mr. Owen, the director of the Hall of Fame, to order pizza for the kids.

While Grace was arranging lunch, the kids continued to wrap. A few minutes later, Mr. Owen walked into the room. He was short and stocky. He looked like a professional wrestler. The kids all stopped wrapping when they saw who was behind him.

It was Big D!

Big D was the Boston Red Sox's best hitter and a favorite of the fans. Mike and Kate had helped find his missing bat when they visited Fenway Park. A man with a video camera followed Big D in. He had a large camera bag slung over his shoulder.

"Hey! Big D! What are you doing here?" Kate asked.

A big smile spread across Big D's face. "Mike! Kate!" he said. *"¡Hola!"*

"¡Feliz Navidad!" Kate said. "Merry Christmas!" She was teaching herself Spanish and always looked for chances to speak it.

Big D walked over to the table and gave Mike, Kate, and all their friends fist bumps.

"It's great to see you! I'm here with my friend Jordan to film a documentary about baseball. We were just in Mr. Owen's office photographing a baseball card."

Big D sat down with the kids and wrapped a present. Then everyone asked him to sign an autograph. Jordan took pictures and videos while he did. Mr. Owen stood off to the side. He checked his watch a few times while Big D talked to the kids.

When Grace walked back into the room, she dropped her purse on the table and looked at Big D. "Hey, Mr. Owen, I thought Big D and Jordan were supposed to be at lunch by now," she said. "They're going to be late!"

Mr. Owen nodded. "I know!" he said. "I was just letting them out, but Big D got sidetracked by his big fans! Come on, time to go!"

Big D stood up and headed for the front

door, but Jordan stopped short. "Hang on," he said to Mr. Owen. "I forgot one of my camera lenses in your office. I'll go get it."

Jordan took off. A moment later, he was back with a big round camera lens in his hand. He unzipped the camera bag hanging from his shoulder and slipped the lens inside. Mr. Owen led him and Big D out the front door.

The kids returned to wrapping. As they got close to finishing, Mike stood up to demonstrate his special batting stance. "Watch this," he said to Caleb. "I've been working on my hitting. I have a new stance to get more power, like Big D!" Mike pretended to hold a bat over his shoulder. He wiggled his hips a few times, and then swung his clenched hands straight into Grace's purse!

The brown leather bag fell to the ground. Coins jingled onto the floor, and a baseball card fell out. A black pen bounced near Mike's feet.

"Oh no!" Mike said. He bent over to pick up the stuff that had spilled. He was just about to reach for the card when Grace grabbed it.

"Got it!" Grace said. She held up a small baseball card with an orange background and an old-fashioned player on it. "I bought this

at the gift shop and was going to wrap it for the kids."

Mike nodded. "That's a Honus Wagner T206 card!" he said. "My dad bought me a copy from the gift shop for my birthday last year."

Grace smiled. "That's why I thought it would make a great gift," she said. Grace placed the card in a gift box and wrapped it in red paper. She tied purple and yellow ribbons around it and put it in the pile of gifts to go under the tree.

Grace clapped her hands. "Okay! Let's finish up before the pizza gets here," she said. The kids scurried to wrap the remaining presents. Then Grace gathered them around the table.

"You did such a great job wrapping the gifts that Mr. Owen has a special reward for you," Grace said. "He told me that after the museum closes tonight, he'll give you a private tour of the Hall of Fame."

The kids cheered. "Cool!" Mike said. He gave Caleb a high five.

Grace help up her hand. "And even better," she said, "while you were wrapping gifts, I checked with all your parents. They gave me approval for something else."

The kids leaned forward. "What?" Kate asked.

"Well, I know you were all going to sleep at Kate's house," Grace said. "But Mr. Owen has invited you to sleep over at the Hall of Fame tonight!"

The kids exploded in cheers!

"Wowee!" Mike yelled. "I'm finally going to make it to the Hall of Fame!"

A Surprising Find

Just after dinner, Mike, Kate, and the rest of the Cooperstown Cares club met back at the Hall of Fame for the sleepover. Mr. Owen led them up to an empty exhibit room on the second floor, where they unrolled their sleeping bags. Mike's sleeping bag was brown and shaped like a baseball glove. Kate's had a picture of a baseball player hitting a ball.

"Hey, we should sing Christmas carols," Mike said as he waited for everyone else to

finish setting up. "Listen to this one. I just made it up!"

Jingle bells, Big D smells
Louie hit a bomb
The Hall of Fame
Blew a game
And Babe Ruth got away!

Caleb and Sophia clapped, but Kate shook her head. "That's not a real Christmas carol!" she said. "How about this one?"

We <u>wish</u> you an extra inning,
We <u>wish</u> you an extra inning,
We <u>wish</u> you an extra inning,
And a lead-off home run!

Mike gave her a high five. "I don't think that's real, either," he said. "But I like them both!"

Mr. Owen clapped his hands for their attention. "It looks like you're all set for the night," he said. "Who would like a private tour of the Hall of Fame?"

Everyone's hands shot up. "We would!" Noah shouted.

Mr. Owen smiled. "Great! Follow me!" he said. "We've got the museum all to ourselves, except for Buddy our security guard. You can say hi to him if we see him. He makes his rounds every twenty minutes."

Mr. Owen led the group through the museum. They started on the third floor with an exhibit about all the different baseball stadiums. But Mike and Kate were most excited when they saw an old friend.

Kate had stopped in front a big glass case that held a full-sized version of the Philadelphia Phillies' mascot. "The Phillie Phanatic!" she said. The mascot was about seven feet tall and covered in green fur. He had a huge cone-shaped nose and wore a Phillies baseball cap.

The rest of the kids gathered around. "When we went to Philadelphia with Kate's mom, we solved the mystery of the fake Phillie Phanatic!" Mike said. He rapped his knuckles on the sturdy glass case. "He locked us in a room, but I guess we got the last laugh!"

For the next hour, the kids enjoyed exploring the museum without any other visitors. Kate stopped at the exhibit of old-time uniforms, including one that Jackie Robinson wore. "They have replica jerseys just like that in the gift shop," Kate said. "I asked for one for Christmas."

"Cool," Mike said. "I asked for a new Cooperstown Crusher bat for Christmas. I bet that will help me hit a home run this year!"

Mr. Owen showed them a Bloopers, Bungles, and Blunders exhibit. The best part was a ten-minute video of baseball players dropping balls, missing catches, running into walls, and generally messing up.

Caleb nudged Mike with his elbow. "Our last game of the season could be on that video!" Caleb said. "Remember you were batting and instead of a home run, you hit a ball that got stuck in the tree behind the plate? We lost big-time to the Utica Aces!"

Mike nodded and laughed. "You're right!" he said. "That *wasn't* a good game. That's why I'm working on my hitting. I really want to beat Utica when we play them in the spring."

"Before we finish," Mr. Owen said, "how would you like to see our Honus Wagner exhibit and maybe even a special baseball card?"

"The Honus Wagner card?" Caleb asked.

"That would be great! It's one of the most expensive baseball cards ever!"

"Yes," Mr. Owen said. "The Honus Wagner card was made in 1909. It's part of the T206 series. There were lots of T206 cards of other players, but not that many Honus Wagner ones, so they're worth a lot of money. In fact, one of the Honus Wagner T206 cards sold for over two million dollars!"

Mr. Owen led them to a small exhibit on the second floor dedicated to Honus Wagner. "Honus Wagner was one of the first five people elected to the Baseball Hall of Fame," Mr. Owen said. "He played twenty-one seasons as shortstop, mostly for the Pittsburgh Pirates. Fans called him the Flying Dutchman because he was so fast."

As they approached the exhibit, Mr. Owen flicked on the overhead lights. The famous card was in a case, along with Honus Wagner's glove and shoes. The kids crowded around it. They took turns studying it.

"It looks just like the reprint card I have at home," Caleb said. "But I wish I had this one."

After everyone had a turn, Mike went back to look some more. Finally, Mr. Owen encouraged him to move along so they could get to sleep.

As the group headed to their sleeping bags, Mike nudged Kate.

"Something's funny," Mike said. "That card looks brand-new. Its edges aren't worn or anything. It doesn't look like it's over one hundred years old."

Kate shrugged. "Maybe it's just a really clean card," she said.

Mike shook his head. "No, that's not it," he said. "I think it's a fake!"

Time to Explore

"Hot chocolate and Christmas cookies!" Kate cheered when the group returned to the area with the sleeping bags.

"That's right," Kate's mother, Mrs. Hopkins, said. "I thought you might want a late-night snack." She had volunteered to stay with the group for the night. Mrs. Hopkins had set up her sleeping bag in the back corner of the room.

"That's a home run," Mike said. He gave her a high five.

Mrs. Hopkins laughed. "Thanks, Mike,"

she said. She started pouring steaming cups of hot chocolate from a thermos. She handed one to Mike. "Here, pass this around the horn to the others. And everyone else, don't get caught looking. Those cookies won't last forever!"

Mike passed out the hot chocolate, while everyone else munched on holiday cookies. As he gave a cup of hot chocolate to Kate, he leaned close to her ear. "Just pretend to go to sleep

tonight," he whispered. "We need to investigate that card after everyone falls asleep."

Kate nodded. "Okay," she whispered.

After a cookie or two, Mr. Owen said good night. "Have a great time with all of my Hall of Fame friends," he said as he headed for the exit. "See you tomorrow morning!"

As Mr. Owen walked away, Mike gathered everyone in a circle. He finished eating a bright green tree cookie, and then wiped his hands on his pants. "Okay, I've got a question for you. What do you call people who are afraid of Santa Claus?"

"Scaredy cats?" Caleb asked. "Or scaredy clauses?"

Mike shook his head. "Good try!" Everyone else was quiet. "Give up?" Mike asked.

"Yup!" Caleb said.

"*Claus*trophobic!" Mike said. "Get it? Like

afraid of small spaces, but with Santa!"

Kate nodded. "Yes, we got it, Mike," she said.

The kids continued to eat and drink and tell jokes until the snacks were gone. Then Mrs. Hopkins told them to put on their pajamas and brush their teeth.

"You wouldn't believe who was watching me!" Scott said when he returned from the bathroom. "There's a huge picture of Babe Ruth downstairs, and his eyes follow you wherever you are in the room. It's really creepy!"

"Cool!" Mike said. "Let's go check it out!"

The kids scampered down the stairs to the picture gallery on the first floor. They took turns walking around as Babe Ruth's eyes followed them.

"That's weird," Caleb said.

"I think it's pretty neat," Kate said. "They

always say that Santa Claus is watching, but now we know that Babe Ruth is watching, too!"

"Maybe Babe Ruth is Santa Claus!" Mike said.

Everyone laughed.

After a few minutes, they walked back upstairs to go to bed. When the kids were tucked into their sleeping bags, Kate's mom flicked off the lights. A red EXIT sign glowed at the far end of the room.

"Good night to all, and to all a good night!" Kate's mom said.

"Good night, Mrs. Hopkins," the kids replied.

Mike and Kate pretended to go to sleep right away. But Caleb started in on the knock-knock jokes.

"Knock-knock!" Caleb said.

"Who's there?" they all asked.

"Mary," Caleb said.

"Mary who?"

"Mary Christmas!" Caleb said, laughing.

"Okay, I got one. I should have said it this morning," Mike said. "Knock-knock!"

"Who's there?" they shouted.

"Rabbit," Mike answered.

"Rabbit who?"

"Rabbit up carefully, it's a present!" Mike snorted.

The jokes continued for a little while, but then Mrs. Hopkins quieted everyone down. They drifted off to sleep one by one.

Mike and Kate waited for Kate's mother to fall asleep. It seemed to take forever. At last, when they heard Mrs. Hopkins snoring, Kate popped up. She carefully stepped over sleeping bags to check that no one else was awake. Then she turned around and gave Mike a thumbs-up. It was time to explore!

Sparklers at the
Hall of Fame

Mike slid out of his sleeping bag. He and Kate tiptoed to the open doorway near the stairs. The museum was pitch-black except for the red EXIT signs.

Mike pulled out a small flashlight and flicked it on. It made a circle of bright white light on the floor. "I brought my rock-hunting flashlight for the sleepover. But we can use it to figure out if that Honus Wagner card is a fake or not," he said. Mike had gotten a rock-collecting book and some tools for his birthday.

"The rock-hunting flashlight will help us spot a fake baseball card?" Kate asked. "Since when did they start making baseball cards out of rocks?"

"It's not a regular flashlight," Mike said. "It's a black-light flashlight! I use it for finding fluorescent minerals in rocks. It has an ultraviolet bulb that makes something glow if it has certain chemicals or minerals in it."

Mike flipped a switch on the flashlight. The circle of white light changed to purple.

"Oh yeah," Kate said. "Like those special markers and lightbulb we got for our haunted house!"

"Exactly," Mike said. "But we can use it to spot fake old-fashioned baseball cards. I learned about it from my dad. We use it at the store all the time to check if old cards really are old.

"After about 1940, companies started adding special chemicals to paper to make them look brighter," Mike said. "If you shine a black light on them, they'll sparkle. But paper older than that won't."

"So if the Honus Wagner card on display is original, it won't sparkle," Kate said.

Mike nodded. But just then, Mike and Kate heard a door shut on the floor below. A moment later, they could hear footsteps coming up the stairs.

"What's that?" Mike asked. "There's no one here except us!"

"Maybe it's a thief!" Kate said. "Quick, we've got to move."

Mike looked around for someplace to run. The entrance to the exhibit halls was on the other side of the stairs. He tugged on Kate's pajama top. "Over there!" he said.

As the footsteps grew louder, Mike and Kate zoomed across the landing to the exhibits. Mike ducked inside. Kate followed. It was dark, but the red EXIT signs gave off just enough light for them to see the edges of things.

The footsteps had made it to the top of the stairs. They had escaped just in time!

Mike and Kate watched as a man flicked a flashlight into the room with their sleeping bags. Kate caught sight of the man just before he turned the flashlight off and started walking again.

"It's not a thief!" Kate said. "It's the security guard, Buddy! Remember, Mr. Owen said he makes his rounds every twenty minutes."

Mike let out a small sigh. "Whew, that makes sense," he said. "But we still can't get caught here! I've got an idea."

They were standing in front of the Babe Ruth exhibit. It was filled with equipment that Babe Ruth had used, including a big locker from Yankee Stadium. Mike hopped inside and pulled Kate in with him. He held his finger in front of his lips to signal for quiet.

The footsteps from the guard grew louder. He was headed straight for them!

Mike and Kate held their breath as the footsteps drew closer. They even heard the guard's breathing when he stopped outside the Babe Ruth exhibit to look around. Mike's lungs felt like they were just about to burst when the guard finally walked on! Slowly, Mike started to breathe again. When they could no longer hear the guard's footsteps, Mike and Kate tumbled out of the locker.

"That was close!" Kate said.

"I know," Mike said. "There's no time to lose.

He'll be back again in twenty minutes. Let's get to the card to investigate."

Mike and Kate quietly wound their way through the museum. They stopped in front of the Honus Wagner exhibit.

Mike pulled out his black-light flashlight. "Watch this!" he said. He flicked the flashlight on. It threw a circle of purple light on the ground. "If that card is real, it shouldn't look any different under black light."

Kate held her breath as Mike flashed the black light on the Honus Wagner exhibit. The shoes, glove, and other items in the Honus Wagner case looked flat and dark blue under the purple light.

But the Honus Wagner card lit up like a sparkler! The white parts of the paper around the edges glowed in the dark.

"Aha!" Mike whispered. "I knew it was fake!"

A Real Fake Card

"Time to wake up!" Mrs. Hopkins called.

One head after another poked out of the sleeping bags scattered across the floor. Mike lifted his head. His hair was messy. He ran his fingers through it. "Is Mr. Owen here yet?" he asked.

"No, not yet," Mrs. Hopkins said. "But the Hall of Fame opens in an hour, and we have to pick up our sleeping bags."

Caleb yawned. "Okay, but I'm hungry," he said.

"That's good," Mrs. Hopkins said. "Mr. Owen is going to bring a big order of Sally's Blue Chip Muffins with him when he comes to work."

Sally's Blue Chip Muffins were a special treat in Cooperstown. They were blueberry muffins with chocolate chips in them.

Caleb pumped his fist in the air. "Score!" he said. "I love Blue Chip Muffins!"

"Then please help clean up and bring your stuff to the research library," Mrs. Hopkins said.

The kids jumped into action. The sleeping bags were rolled up in no time at all. Everyone grabbed their

backpacks and sleeping bags and followed Mrs. Hopkins to the Hall of Fame's research library.

As soon as they pushed the door to the library open, the smell of blueberries and chocolate hit them.

"Dig in!" Mr. Owen said. He stood behind the long research table in the middle of the room. Spread across the top of it were plates, big piles of muffins, bananas, strawberries, and glasses of orange juice.

The kids crowded the table and heaped their plates with muffins and fruit. As soon as they sat down to eat, the talk turned to Christmas presents.

"I asked for a new baseball glove and some special oil to soften it up," Caleb said. "My dad said to rub oil in the palm of the glove. Put a baseball in and wrap it tight with a rubber band. Then you put it under your mattress and it will mold itself into the perfect shape for catching balls. If I break the glove in over the winter, it'll be perfect for spring."

"I asked for a pitch-back," Scott said. "When the snow is gone, I'll use it to work on my fielding. And my dad said we might be able to set it up in the basement."

While the others were talking about presents, Mike nudged Kate. He nodded in the direction of Mr. Owen, who was eating with Kate's mom.

"Keep an eye on him," Mike whispered. "Let's talk to him when he's finished with breakfast."

"Good idea," she said.

For the rest of the meal, everyone swapped stories about Christmas morning, Santa Claus, and holidays. The kids were jealous of Caleb when he said that he got eight days of presents

for Hanukkah. Then Rani told them her family made sweet treats like pineapple tarts for the Muslim holiday of Eid, after Ramadan. That made Mike and Tommy hungry enough to grab more muffins.

When they finished eating, everyone got up and threw their trash away. But instead of heading back to the table, Mike and Kate walked over to Mr. Owen's office. He was on the phone, so they waited outside his door. When Mr. Owen finished his call, Kate poked her head in.

"Oh, hello!" Mr. Owen said. "Come in!" He was sitting behind his desk on the far side of the room. Grace was there, too. She was sipping coffee and working at her desk. Next to her was a special table with a clean white background for taking pictures of museum pieces.

"Thanks for all your help yesterday," Grace said. "The kids will really appreciate those gifts. I just wish we could have raised more money this year to help build a new community center."

"You're welcome. It was fun," Kate said. "But we have some bad news for Mr. Owen. Mike and I discovered something that we think you should know about."

"Oh?" he said, raising an eyebrow. "What's going on?"

Mike stepped forward. "The Honus Wagner card on display is a fake!" he said.

Mr. Owen nodded, and his face relaxed.

Mike glanced at Kate. "Did you hear me?" he asked. "Someone's stolen your Honus Wagner card!"

Mr. Owen smiled. "Yes, I heard you, and you're right!" he said. Mr. Owen waved his hand. "The Honus Wagner card in that display case *is* a fake!"

"What do you mean?" Mike and Kate asked. "You've been robbed? That card is worth millions!"

"No, that's not what happened," Mr. Owen said with a smile. "When Big D and Jordan were at the Hall of Fame yesterday making their video, they needed a shot of the Honus Wagner card. So we took the original card out of the display case and put in one of the replica cards from the gift shop. We brought the *real* one back here."

He pointed to the table next to Grace's desk. "Jordan photographed it there. Then I put it in the safe for the night. I was going to put it back on display after breakfast," he said. "How did you realize that the card on display was a fake?"

"We shined Mike's black-light flashlight on it," Kate said. "And the paper sparkled, so we know it's not from 1909!"

"That's a pretty good piece of detective work," Mr. Owen said. "We've used black light here at the Hall of Fame to double-check old cards. Would you like to see the real Honus Wagner baseball card now?"

"Yes!" Mike and Kate said.

Mr. Owen went to the safe in his office and spun the dial back and forth. The heavy metal door swung open, and he reached in and took a box out of the safe. He set the box on the table next to Grace.

Grace glanced over. "Here, let me move my stuff out of the way," she said. She pulled some of her papers closer to her desk.

Mr. Owen opened the box's hinged cover. The inside was lined in bright green felt. In the middle of the green felt was the real Honus Wagner card!

Mike and Kate peeked into the box. "Wow!" Kate said. "I can't believe that small piece of paper is worth millions of dollars!"

"It's just so rare," Mr. Owen said. "That's

why they're worth so much. We have to be careful to keep them in perfect condition. We always make sure that no one touches this card without special gloves on."

Mike leaned over to get a closer look at the card. Then he took out his flashlight and set it on black-light mode. He closed the cover of the box as much as he could and then shined the light inside.

"What are you doing, Mike?" Mr. Owen asked.

Mike put down the flashlight and opened the lid of the box. "I'll show you," he said. Then Mike reached into the box and picked the card up.

"Mike!" Mr. Owen said. "That's priceless! You're going to ruin it!"

A Suspect

Mike held up the Honus Wagner T206 card. "It's not priceless," he said. "It's worthless!"

Mr. Owen stepped forward to take the card from Mike. "You really can't do that," he said. "This is an important baseball artifact!"

"No, it's not," said Mike. "It's a fake!"

"What?" asked Grace. "How could it be a fake?"

Mike handed the card to Mr. Owen. "It's one of the reproduction cards from the gift shop," he said. "You can tell because the edges are so straight and clean. And when I shined the black light on it, the paper lit up like a sparkler!"

Mr. Owen peered closely at the card. He gasped and dropped the card on the table. "You're right. This is a fake!" he said. "The real Honus Wagner card has been stolen!"

"How could that be?" Grace asked. "I thought the safe was impossible to break into!"

Mr. Owen walked over and looked at the safe. There was no sign that anyone had tried to break into it.

"Well, someone must have switched a fake card with the real one between when you took it out of the display case and when you put it in the safe," Kate said.

"But how?" Mr. Owen asked. "I was with Big D and Jordan and the card the whole time! When we were done taking pictures of the card, I put it away. There wasn't time for anyone to steal it. I don't know how this could have happened." Mr. Owen sank into his chair. "This is terrible! I will lose my job!"

Kate stood up. "Let's go over what happened yesterday," she said. She pointed at Mr. Owen. "You were showing Big D and Jordan around the museum. They needed a shot of the Honus Wagner card, so you took it out of the display case and brought it back here to the office."

Kate pointed at the special table. "You put the card there, and Jordan took pictures of it, right?"

"Yes," Mr. Owen said. He glanced at Grace. "You had just come in to order pizza. You watched them photograph the card, right? Nothing happened to it then."

Grace nodded. "Yup," she said. "I saw it. I was there."

"What happened after that?" Kate asked.

Mr. Owen stood up. He pointed to a pair of white cotton gloves on the photography table. "When Jordan finished taking pictures of the Honus Wagner card, I put those gloves on and put the card into its box. Then I put it in the safe," he said.

Grace smacked her hand on the table and jumped up. "That's it!" she said. "You didn't put it right in the safe! When Big D and Jordan

were done with the pictures, they were late for lunch. So you let them out the front door, and I went to wrap presents. You waited to put the card away until you got back!"

"But that doesn't tell us who stole it," Mr. Owen said.

Grace smiled. "Yes, it does," she said. "We were all wrapping presents just before Jordan and Big D left for lunch. But can you remember who ran back to your office?"

"Jordan!" Kate said. "He went to get his camera lens!"

Grace clapped her hands. "Exactly!" she said. "And I'll bet that's when Jordan stole the Honus Wagner card!"

"Jordan?" Mr. Owen asked. "I can't believe that Jordan would have stolen the card. He used to work for me. I can vouch for him. Someone else must have done it."

"I don't know," Grace said. "Jordan was the only person who went back into the office."

"I just don't think it was him," Mr. Owen said. "Maybe someone stole it after Jordan left, when I was showing him and Big D to the front door. It probably took me five minutes to get back to my office. That makes more sense than Jordan taking the card."

"We were all in the research library wrapping presents at that time," Grace said. "I didn't see anyone else. It seems like the police should start by questioning Jordan. Are he and Big D still in Cooperstown?"

"Yes, they're not leaving for a couple days," Mr. Owen said. "They're staying at the Otesaga."

The Otesaga was Cooperstown's famous old hotel. It was a few blocks from the Hall of Fame and sat on the edge of Otsego Lake. The hotel had columns in the front and a big porch in the back that overlooked the lake. Lots of famous baseball players had stayed there for Hall of Fame events.

Mike sprang up from his chair. "Well, let's go investigate!" he said.

Mr. Owen shook his head. "No, we can leave that to the police," he said. "Plus, Jordan just couldn't have stolen the card. I know he's a good guy."

"What if you issued a reward for the return of the card?" Grace asked. "I'll bet if you offered some money, whoever took it might return it. A reward might be a really good idea."

Mr. Owen tapped the desk with his fingers. "That *is* a good idea, Grace," he said. "I'll need to get approval for that. But first, I've got to call the police so they can handle it."

"Okay," Mike said. He tugged on Kate's

shirt. "Come on, Kate. We need to help clean up. Good luck!"

As soon as they left Mr. Owen's office, Mike pulled Kate aside. "We need to get to Jordan before the police do," he said. "I think he stole the card. But Mr. Owen seems to trust him. We need to investigate."

The Real Thief

After breakfast, Kate's mom gave them permission to go to the Otesaga to visit with Big D and Jordan.

As Mike and Kate ran down Cooperstown's main street, their boots crunched on the light blanket of snow. They passed green wreaths hung on lampposts and stores decorated for the holidays.

Mike pulled open the front door of the Otesaga. The lobby was covered with ropes of green garland and colorful ornaments. It

looked ready for the big community center holiday party that night.

"Where do you think Jordan is?" Kate asked as they looked around the lobby.

"Well, he's definitely not here," Mike said. "Let's start by checking the gift shop, the reading room, and the business center."

They ran to the gift shop and then the reading room, but Jordan wasn't in either. Then Mike and Kate headed for the business center. It was a small room that had three computers and a printer.

"Bingo!" Mike said as they walked in. Jordan was writing on a pad next to one of the computers.

Jordan looked up when they entered the room. "Hi, kids," he said.

"Hi!" Kate said. She and Mike sat down in two of the empty chairs nearby. "You have a minute? We just came from the Hall of Fame and had a question about yesterday."

"Sure," Jordan said. "What's up?"

Mike glanced at Kate. "When you went back for your camera lens, did you take anything else out of Mr. Owen's office?" Mike asked.

Jordan raised his eyebrows. "No! I just took

my lens," he said. "Why? What's missing?"

"We can't say," Kate said. "But Mr. Owen can't find something that was in the office yesterday, and we wondered if you had taken it."

Jordan sighed and shook his head. "Well, I didn't take anything out of that office except for my camera lens," he said. He tucked his pad and pen into a large camera bag at his feet and stood up. He picked up the bag and slung it over his shoulder. "I need to get going. Good luck."

Jordan disappeared out the door.

Mike and Kate looked at each other. "What was that about?" Kate asked. "He seemed nervous!"

Mike put his feet up on the table. "I don't know," he said. "But he sure got out of here quick, like he had something to hide. I told you he took the card!"

Kate leaned against the desk. "If he took it, where did he put it?" she asked. Kate thought for a minute. "Probably in his room! I wonder if there's any way we could search it."

"Not without breaking in," Mike said. He tapped the desk. Then he snapped his fingers. "But hey, maybe we don't need to!"

"What do you mean?" Kate asked.

"Remember when I found that really rare quarter last year?" Mike asked. "I kept it in my pocket the whole week until I could go to the coin shop on Saturday. The Honus Wagner card is worth a lot more than my quarter. I'll bet Jordan has it with him, just like I did!"

"But if we can't search his room, we definitely can't search his pockets!" she said.

Mike shook his head. "We don't need to," he said. "It's not in his pocket. What did he grab just before he left?"

Kate twirled a strand of her hair between her fingers. "His *camera bag*!" she said.

"Exactly," Mike said. "All we have to do is find him, and then one of us can distract him while the other looks through his camera bag for the card!"

"That's a great idea. Let's go," Kate said. She stood up. "We'll check the lobby first."

Mike popped out of his chair and followed Kate into the hallway.

When they reached the lobby, they scanned the room for Jordan. But there was no sign of him. "Let's check the workout room downstairs," Mike said.

They headed for the elevators. Kate pushed the DOWN button. *BING!* The elevator chimed, and its doors opened.

Mike jumped in. But before Kate could step inside, they heard a man's voice from the lobby. "Mike and Kate! Wait!"

Mike looked up. Kate turned around.

It was Jordan! He was walking toward the elevator.

"I've got something to tell you," he said as he stopped in front of them.

Mike hopped off the elevator. The doors clanged shut behind him.

"I'm glad I caught you two," Jordan said. He ran his hand through his hair and scratched the back of his head.

Mike glanced at Kate. She shrugged.

"You were right," Jordan said. He looked down at the floor. "I did take something else from the office yesterday."

Mike's and Kate's eyes widened. "You did?" Kate asked. "Why didn't you tell us?"

"I don't know. You surprised me when you asked about it," Jordan said. "I didn't know what to do. But after I left, I realized I should tell the truth."

"That's good," Mike said. "So what happened?"

Jordan rubbed his hands together. "When I went back to get my lens, I saw something on Mr. Owen's desk that I couldn't resist. I just had to take it," he said. "I didn't think it was a big deal. Maybe you can tell Mr. Owen that I'm sorry."

Kate nodded. "We'll tell him," she said. "But do you still have the baseball card?"

Jordan looked at Kate. "Baseball card?" he asked. "I didn't take a baseball card. I took a Christmas cookie!"

"A Christmas cookie?" Mike and Kate both said.

"Yes, there was a bag of them on the desk," Jordan said. "And I didn't think Mr. Owen would mind. But I should have asked first."

"So you didn't take the Honus Wagner card?" Kate asked.

Jordan straightened up. "No! I didn't take that!" he said. "Why? Is it missing? It's worth a fortune!"

"Someone stole the Honus Wagner card and replaced it with a fake," Mike said. "It happened after you and Big D photographed it and before Mr. Owen came back from showing you to the door. We thought you might have stolen it because you were the only one who was alone in the office during that time."

"It wasn't me!" he said. He rocked back on his heels and thought for a moment. "I *was* alone with the card when I went to get my lens.

But there was someone else who was alone with it besides me."

"There was?" Kate asked.

"Who?" Mike asked.

"Grace!" Jordan said.

"What?" Kate asked. "Are you sure?"

"Positive," he said. "We went to Mr. Owen's office to photograph the Honus Wagner card. Mr. Owen and Big D watched me. Then Grace came in and ordered pizza. When I finished photographing the card, we all started to leave. Mr. Owen and Big D left first. I was going to hold the door open for Grace, but then she said to go ahead. She had to look for her purse and she'd be out in a minute. She stayed behind after I left."

"That's interesting," Mike said. "Thanks for the info."

"Anytime," Jordan said. "I hope you find it!"

Kate and Mike headed for the door. As soon as they were out of earshot, Kate turned to Mike.

"Well, we can't prove that Jordan didn't take the card," she said. "But now we know that Grace was alone in the office with it. You know what that means, right?"

Mike nodded. "Yup," he said. "If Jordan is telling the truth, then Grace is our next suspect!"

Unwrapping
a Surprise

"Wow!" Kate said. She tapped Mike on the chest with her finger. "And you know what? If Grace *did* steal the Honus Wagner card, I might have an idea where it is!"

Mike's eyes popped open. "You do?" he asked. "Where?"

"The Hall of Fame!" Kate said. "Remember? You almost held it in your hands!"

"What do you mean?" Mike asked. "When?"

"You spilled Grace's purse when we were wrapping presents yesterday," Kate said. "The

Honus Wagner card that fell out was the real one! You were about to pick it up, but then Grace grabbed it."

"I thought that was just a copy!" Mike exclaimed. "She said she got it at the gift shop to donate."

Kate nodded. "I know! But what if she was lying? She probably bought a Honus Wagner card at the gift shop earlier that day. Maybe she slipped the fake one into the box in the office when she took the real one and put it in her purse!"

"How would she have known she'd have a chance to steal the card when everyone left the office?" Mike asked.

Kate shook her head. "She didn't. I think she was probably just going to donate the Honus Wagner card from the gift shop," she said. "But when everyone left and the card was sitting there, I'll bet she suddenly decided to swap it with the fake one she had just bought!"

Mike let out a low whistle. "That's sneaky," he said.

"When you spilled her purse, the stolen card fell out. She had to say it was a gift and wrap it up so it wouldn't look strange," Kate said. "We've got to find that present!"

Mike and Kate rushed through the snow to the Hall of Fame.

They waved to Ella, the woman at the ticket booth. "We're just helping with the holiday toy drive," Kate said. "We want to check out a few of the presents that we wrapped yesterday."

Ella nodded and waved them in. "Have fun," she said. "It's a slow day today. We haven't had many visitors this morning."

Kate stopped. "Oh, one other thing," she said. "Have you seen Grace lately?"

Ella thought for a moment. "She was here earlier," she said. "But she left for lunch about twenty minutes ago."

"Thanks!" Mike said. He and Kate zipped into the Hall of Fame gallery. The presents they had wrapped the day before were still under the tree.

"I hope she didn't take it when she left for lunch," Kate said. They rushed over to the tree. "Look for a present wrapped in red paper with two ribbons on it. I noticed she put a yellow ribbon and a purple ribbon on the gift she wrapped yesterday. She must have done that so she could find it again."

Mike and Kate dug through the pile looking for the gift. They sorted through all the presents but didn't find any with double ribbons.

Mike leaned against the wall. "It's gone!" he said.

Kate nodded. "She must have smuggled it out of the building," she said. "Unless . . ."

Kate tapped the ground with her foot.

Mike straightened up. "Unless what?" he asked.

"Unless she just moved it somewhere else," Kate said. "Like her office! Let's go!"

Mike and Kate ran through the hallway connecting the Hall of Fame to the research library and offices in the back. They pushed the library door open and walked over to Mr. Owen's office. Kate peeked in. It was empty.

"Quick!" she said. She and Mike slipped into the office. It looked just like it had that morning. They scanned the room, but there was no present anywhere.

Kate's shoulders slumped. "I thought for sure we'd find it here," she said. "I guess it's gone for good."

She had just started for the door when Mike tapped her back. "Not so fast," he said. "I think I found it!"

Kate turned around. "Where?" she asked.

"I'll show you," Mike said. "Hang on." He took out his phone and held it up to take a picture.

"What are you doing?" Kate asked. "We're not sightseeing!"

Mike pointed to a paper bag on the floor under Grace's desk. "I'm taking a picture of evidence," he said. Mike picked up the

bag. Inside was a present wrapped in red paper with two ribbons!

"Got it," Mike said softly.

Kate leaned over to look as Mike carefully slipped the wrapping off the white gift box.

Mike lifted the top of the box, and they let out a gasp.

A Surprising Gift

Inside the box was a Honus Wagner card!

"Here, hold this," Mike said. He handed the box to Kate. Then he reached into his pocket and pulled out his flashlight. Mike slipped the cover of the box mostly back on and shined the flashlight inside.

The Honus Wagner card didn't sparkle. It was the real one!

"You'd better be careful," Mike said. "That's a two-million-dollar baseball card you're holding! We've got to get it to Mr. Owen!" He started to take the box from Kate's hand.

"Not yet!" Kate said. "Even though we saw her wrap the card, we can't prove that she took it. I know how we can trap her! Quick, go get one of those extra gift boxes from yesterday. They're in the hallway!"

Mike returned a minute later with a box in one hand and a roll of green ribbon in the other.

"Thanks," Kate said. "But we only need the box. Let me have it."

Mike handed her the empty box. Then Kate gave him the box with the real Honus Wagner card. She slipped the empty one into the red wrapping paper and taped it up. When she was done, Kate tied on the yellow and purple ribbons.

Kate placed the empty present back in the bag and put it under Grace's desk. Kate searched the desk for a blank piece of paper

and wrote a note. When she was done, she
showed it to Mike.

We know you took the Honus Wagner card.
We even know where it is.
You don't.
It's time to give yourself up.

Kate folded the note and grabbed an

envelope from the desk. She stuffed the note inside and sealed it. Then she wrote Grace's name on the front.

"We have to give this to Ella before Grace gets back from lunch," Kate said. She took the box with the real Honus Wagner card from Mike and headed for the door. "Come on!"

Mike followed Kate as she ran to the front entrance. Kate slowed down and walked up to Ella.

"Can you give this to Grace when she returns from lunch?" Kate asked. "But please don't tell her who gave it to you. It's a surprise."

Ella nodded. "Sure thing," she said.

"Thanks," Kate said. She pulled Mike to the big holiday tree in the middle of the Hall of Fame gallery. She walked to the far side of the tree and stopped.

Mike looked around. "Okay, what are we doing here?" he asked.

"This is the perfect spot to wait for Grace," she said. "As soon as she comes back from lunch, Ella will give her that note. She'll get nervous and rush back to her office to check for the Honus Wagner card. She'll have to walk right past this tree on the way. We'll hide here and then follow her when she does."

For twenty minutes, they hid behind the tree and waited. While Kate was keeping an eye out for Grace, Mike wound and unwound the roll of green ribbon on his fingers.

"It's her!" Kate whispered. She nudged Mike with her elbow. "Move a little bit to the right as she walks by. And put that ribbon away!"

Mike hurried to unwind the ribbon from his fingers. As Grace walked quickly past the tree, he and Kate shifted around to the other side so she wouldn't see them. Grace had Kate's note in her hand. She kept glancing at the note and looking around as she walked. She was definitely in a hurry.

"Now!" Kate said. She and Mike followed Grace around the corner. When she went into the office, Mike and Kate crept up to the edge of the door and peeked inside. Mike pulled out his phone to take pictures for evidence.

Grace dropped her purse and Kate's note on her desk. Then she bent down and grabbed the bag with the gift in it. She quickly pulled the wrapped present out. Mike snapped a picture of her holding it.

She slipped the ribbons off just like Mike had done and unwrapped the gift. As soon as the paper fell away, Grace lifted the cover off of the box. Then she gasped out loud.

"Oh no!" she exclaimed. She rattled the box and turned it upside down. The bed of cotton on the bottom fluttered to the ground. The box was empty!

"Oh no! Oh no! Oh no!" Grace said quietly.

Kate nudged Mike. Then they stepped forward.

"Looking for this?" Kate asked. She held out the box she had been carrying and took the cover off. The orange Honus Wagner card was easy to spot. Grace looked at them, and then at the empty box in her hand.

"Um, what are you talking about?" she said. "Why do you have that card? Have you been spying on me?"

"Yes, because you've been stealing baseball cards!" Mike asked. "Like this real Honus Wagner T206. We want to know why it was under your desk!"

Grace looked confused and upset. But she popped up and lunged at Kate and the card. "I need that back!" she said. "Give it to me!"

Kate ducked. As Grace tried to grab the card, Mike quickly whipped out the ribbon he had been playing with and wrapped it tightly around her hands.

"What are you doing?" she said. "This is all a mistake!"

"No, it isn't!" Kate said. "But it was a mistake for you to steal the Honus Wagner card. Now we've caught you red-handed!"

Honus Comes Home

Grace's lip quivered. "No, you didn't!" she said. "How could I steal the card if it was here? That card has never been out of this building." She struggled to loosen her hands from the ribbons but couldn't.

As Grace twisted her hands back and forth, footsteps echoed in the hallway. Mr. Owen appeared from around the corner. He stopped suddenly and looked at Grace with her hands tied up in green ribbon.

"What's going on?" he asked. "Is this some kind of a joke?"

Grace glared at Mr. Owen. "I don't know," she said. "These kids are playing a game. They thought it would be funny to trap me."

"We're not playing any game," Kate said. "Stealing artifacts from the Hall of Fame is serious business." She took a step toward Mr. Owen. "I think you'll want this back."

Kate handed Mr. Owen the gift box she had been holding. He slipped the cover off and his eyes grew wide.

"It's the real Honus Wagner card! I can tell by its edges," he said. "Where did you get it?"

Kate pointed to Grace. "She stole it when you left your office to let Big D and Jordan out," she said.

"But I thought she left with us," Mr. Owen said.

"She didn't," Mike said. "We talked to Jordan this morning. He said Grace stayed behind to look for her purse. That's when she stole the card."

Mr. Owen shook his head. "I can't believe this," he said.

Grace pulled her shoulders back. "Then don't!" she said. She pointed at Mike and Kate. "They're making this up!"

"No, we're not," Mike said. He took out his phone and clicked on it until a picture of Grace's desk came up on the screen. "The stolen card was in this bag, on the floor! We took a picture of it there half an hour ago. Who else would put it there?"

Mr. Owen studied the picture. Mike held it up for Grace to see.

Grace looked at the floor for a moment, and a big smile broke across her face. "Well, of course I did it," she said. "When I heard the real one was missing this morning, I happened to remember that one of the kids wrapped a Honus Wagner card yesterday. I was worried that it might have been the real one. So I fished it out of the present pile and put it under my desk for safekeeping. I was going to give it to you after lunch to check."

Mike and Kate looked at each other. "That's a lie!" Kate said. "You might have taken that present out of the pile this morning, but *you're* the one who wrapped it yesterday." Kate pointed to the red wrapping paper and the purple and yellow ribbons on the floor that Grace had torn off the gift a few minutes before.

"I watched you! You wrapped that Honus Wagner card that fell out of your purse in red wrapping paper and used two ribbons so you could find it later!" Kate said.

Mike flipped through all the pictures he took of Grace opening the present.

Mr. Owen stared at the photos and then at Grace. "You've always been such a good person, Grace!" he said. "Why would you do this? Did you need money that badly?"

Grace looked at Mike's phone, at the wrapping paper and ribbons on the ground, and then at Mr. Owen. She let out a little sigh.

"I'm sorry," she said in a soft voice. "Mike and Kate are right. I did steal the card."

"Why?" Mr. Owen said. "Why would you steal from us?"

"It was for the kids," Grace said. "We don't have enough money for the community center. I thought if I stole the card, someone would offer reward money. Then I could turn the card in and donate the money. You'd get your card back, and the kids would get a new community center. It would be good for everyone!"

"But that's stealing!" Mr. Owen said.

"I know," Grace said. "I've never stolen anything in my life. But when you left that two-million-dollar baseball card sitting in the office yesterday, I just took it without thinking."

"And then you left it here, under the tree," Kate said. "Why didn't you take it home?"

"I had second thoughts after I took it, but

I didn't know how to put it back without getting in trouble," Grace said. "When it fell on the floor, I just figured I'd wrap it and leave it here. I knew it was safe, and I could figure out what to do later.

"I know it was wrong," she pleaded. "That's why I came back today and put the present in the office. I was going to find a way to give it back."

Mr. Owen nodded. "I see," he said. He looked at the Honus Wagner card in his hand. Then he walked over to the safe and put it inside. After he closed the door and spun the dial, he turned around.

"Okay, the card is safe. We should take those ribbons off now," he said.

Kate used a pair of scissors sitting on the desk to cut the green ribbons off Grace's wrists.

"I'm so sorry!" Grace said. "It was all for the kids. I was never going to sell the Honus Wagner card or damage it. I just needed to find a way to raise more money!"

"I'm afraid you're going to have to tell that to the police," Mr. Owen said. He picked up the phone. "We can all just wait right here to tell them the whole story."

"But the holiday party is tonight!" Grace said. "I have to take the gifts to the Otesaga right now, or none of the kids will get any presents!"

"Sit down, Grace," Mr. Owen said. "You're not going anywhere except to the police station. But maybe Mike and Kate can get the presents there."

"How can we bring all those presents?" Kate said. "We can't drive yet!"

Mike nudged her. "But my dad can!" he said. "He has a big van for his sporting goods store. We can load the presents in it and bring them over in one trip! I'll give him a call."

Big D's Plan

"We did it!" Mike said. He stepped back from the holiday tree set up in the ballroom of the Otesaga. It was five o'clock and the kids had just started arriving for the party. With the help of Mike's dad, he and Kate had moved the presents from the Hall of Fame to the hotel.

Kate nodded. "I'm glad we got all the presents here in time," she said.

Mike looked startled. "*Almost* all the presents," he said. "I forgot one! Wait here. I need to catch my dad before he leaves!"

Mike ran out the door. Kate watched the kids examine the frosted cookies on the table at the side of the room. When Mike came back, he was carrying a big flat present.

Kate pointed to the tree. "Hurry up and get it under there!" she said.

Mike shook his head. "Nope. It's not going under the tree," he said. He handed the present to Kate. "This one's for you! I wanted to thank you and your parents for bringing us to so many baseball stadiums. I've had so much fun!"

Kate smiled. She tore into the red-and-white wrapping paper.

It was a framed map of all the major-league baseball stadiums. And near each one they visited, Mike had pasted a picture of him and Kate at the stadium! "I love it!" Kate said.

She gave him a big hug. Then she reached into her bag and pulled out a small gift-wrapped package. She handed it to Mike.

He tore into the bright green wrapping paper to reveal a box. He lifted the lid and pulled out a colorful bracelet with a hologram in the middle.

"It's a power bracelet," Kate said. "It's designed to give you more power and balance when you're at bat. I thought it would help you hit better!"

Mike slipped it on his wrist. Then he took a couple of air swings. "It feels great!" he said. "I think I'm stronger already! I feel like Big D!"

"Well, that's good," Kate said. "Because as part of my present, Big D's going to give you a batting lesson, too! My mother arranged for him to meet you at the batting cages tomorrow. He said he'd give you some secret tips for

hitting home runs!"

Mike smiled and hugged Kate. "Thank you!" he said. "That will be amazing! What a great Christmas!"

"And hey, that reminds me!" Kate said. "We need to find Big D and Jordan to tell them that we found the Honus Wagner card!"

Mike nodded. "Let's check at the front desk," he said.

He and Kate ran through the long corridors of the hotel to the lobby. Mike asked the woman behind the counter about Big D. "Check the reading room," she said. "It's just around the corner."

Mike and Kate ran over to the reading room. Its walls were lined with books, and the windows gave a nice view of the snow-covered lake and mountains. Big D and Jordan were sitting at a table playing cards. Big D looked up when they came into the room. He held up his hand.

SMACK! SMACK! Mike and Kate high-fived with Big D.

"Did Jordan tell you that the Honus Wagner card at the Hall of Fame was stolen yesterday?" Kate asked.

"Yes!" Big D said. "I couldn't believe it when he told me. It's such a famous card. Will they be able to get it back?"

"Yup, don't worry," Mike said. "We just found it! It's back in Mr. Owen's safe now."

"That's great!" Big D said. "But how did it get there?"

"Grace took it. She was trying to play Robin Hood, taking from the Hall of Fame to give to the community center," Kate said. She explained to Big D how she and Mike had tracked down the missing card.

"Oh," Big D said. "That's not good. Grace shouldn't have stolen it."

"You're right," Kate said. "Grace will be in trouble for stealing it. But the kids in Cooperstown will also be in trouble because now Grace can't raise any more money."

Big D nodded. "That's too bad for the kids," he said. Then he stood up and stretched.

"Are you coming to the party?" Mike asked. "It's starting soon."

"I sure will," he said. "But I've got an idea to make the party a bit more fun! Let me make a few calls, and then I'll be down. Keep the hot chocolate warm for me!"

The party was in full swing when Mike and Kate made it back. The room was filled with kids from the community center. They were playing Pin the Star on the Tree and a mystery stocking game, where kids had to guess what was stuffed inside colorful stockings. All the presents were stacked under the tree in the middle of the room.

Mike and Kate stopped at the cookies and milk table. Kate picked up a butterscotch haystack cookie, while Mike poured himself a hot chocolate and grabbed a crispy chocolate stick cookie.

"This is great!" Kate said. "I wonder when Santa is going to come."

Mike looked at the time. "He should be here soon," he said. Mike pointed to a door in the back of the room. "I think he's supposed to come through there."

Mike and Kate continued to munch their cookies while the kids had fun playing holiday games. "I guess Santa is missing!" Mike said. "Maybe Rudolph lost his way."

Just then, the door in the back swung open!

"That must be Santa!" Kate said.

"Hmphfffff," Mike said. He was busy chewing on a cookie.

At first, it looked like Santa! But when Mike and Kate looked more closely, it was something better.

It was Big D dressed up as Santa!

Big D had a red Santa suit on, and a fluffy white beard. He carried a bag over his shoulder. Jordan trailed behind, taking pictures.

The kids cheered and started chanting, "Big D! Big D! Big D!" He waved, and then sat on a chair at the front of the room. One by one, Big D handed out the presents.

When he was done, Big D stood and held up his hands for quiet.

"I hope you enjoy the presents, but I've got some special news," he said. "I heard about how much you kids need a new community

center. And I know someone who tried a little too hard to get money for it. So I called a few of my baseball friends."

Mike and Kate looked at each other. "That must be why he was late," Kate said.

Big D continued. "I called players on the Yankees, the Dodgers, the Cubs, and a bunch of other teams," he said. "And they all agreed

that they'd chip in money to build a new community center for Cooperstown!"

The kids exploded in cheers. Mike and Kate clapped and jumped up and down.

Big D waved his hands again for quiet. "But there was one condition that everyone required before they would donate money," Big D said. "And it's an important one."

The room went silent.

"We all agreed to donate the money, but only if we can also give enough to make a new baseball field for the town team!" Big D said.

The room exploded in cheers a second time! Mike and Kate cheered, too. A huge smile crossed Big D's face. He waved again, and then stepped over to Mike and Kate.

"You two did a great job finding that missing card!" Big D said.

"Thanks," said Mike.

"And it sounds like you did a great job tracking down some of your friends to help the kids of Cooperstown," Kate said. "That's pretty special!"

"It seemed like the right thing to do," Big D said. "I'm glad the other players and I were able to help out. It feels so good to do something for someone else!"

Mike raised his hand. "Good job!" he said.

Big D leaned over. *SMACK!* He gave Mike a high five. Then he turned to Kate. *SMACK!* He gave her one, too.

Big D straightened back up and patted his large red Santa belly. "I know this is Santa's gig," he said. "But ho, ho, ho! Merry Christmas and happy holidays to everyone!"

Dugout Notes

☆ Cooperstown ☆ and the National Baseball Hall of Fame

Honus at the Hall. Exhibits change at the National Baseball Hall of Fame all the time, but the Hall has two original 1909 Honus Wagner T206 cards. One is usually on display. Their value is not displayed with the cards, but other Honus Wagner cards have sold for more than $3 million.

The first five. The first five players voted into the Hall of Fame were Ty Cobb, Walter Johnson, Christy Mathewson, Babe Ruth, and Honus Wagner, in 1936. The first Induction (or welcoming) Ceremony was held on June 12, 1939. The author's father, Kevin Kelly, attended it as a little boy with his father. He was impressed with Connie Mack, a great manager who always wore a suit.

Doubtful Doubleday. In 1905, the Mills Commission, a group of baseball experts, was formed to decide who invented baseball. Without much

 evidence, they announced that Civil War General Abner Doubleday invented baseball in Cooperstown, New York, around 1839. However, it's unlikely that Doubleday had anything to do with baseball.

Why Cooperstown? Whether it was true or not, once the legend of Abner Doubleday inventing baseball took hold, the people of Cooperstown decided to celebrate the town's alleged connection to baseball. They bought Elihu Phinney's cow pasture, where Doubleday supposedly invented baseball, and turned it into a baseball park in 1920. By the 1930s, a movement grew for creating a baseball museum and hall of fame in Cooperstown. The National Baseball Hall of Fame and Museum opened in 1939.

Town-ball. The real origin of baseball has been debated for over one hundred years. Baseball is similar to rounders, an English game played with a ball and bat and four bases. The word *baseball* first appeared in 1744 in an English children's book. Baseball was known by other names, including town-ball, round-ball, and base-ball. Around 1850, official rules were created and

the modern form of baseball started to take shape.

How to get into the Hall. Baseball players are elected into the Hall of Fame by baseball writers and reporters. Players need to have played in the major leagues for at least ten years. They have to wait five years after they are done playing before they are eligible for the Hall of Fame. Baseball writers vote for their top ten eligible players each year. Any player who gets more than 75 percent of votes is accepted.

Cooperstown confidential. Cooperstown is in the middle of New York State.

It's surrounded by farmland, a beautiful lake, and rugged mountains. It was home to James Fenimore Cooper, a famous writer who wrote a book called *The Last of the Mohicans*. The town was named after his father, the founder. Today the town is filled with baseball- and vacation-related stores. Lots of baseball teams come to play on historic Doubleday Field or at a large set of baseball fields outside of town.

Stone giant. A fun place to visit in Cooperstown is the Farmers' Museum. The museum recreates farm life from the 1800s. Visitors can explore two dozen historic buildings, including a general store, a blacksmith's shop, and a doctor's office. But one of the most interesting exhibits is the Cardiff Giant. The Cardiff Giant is one of the country's biggest hoaxes! The ten-foot-tall "petrified" man was discovered in 1869 by workers digging a well on a farm. The farm owner started charging people fifty cents to see it and was soon making lots of money. Then P. T. Barnum made his own Cardiff Giant and started showing it. Eventually both were revealed as fakes, but not until lots of people had paid to see them.

Otsego to Glimmerglass. Cooperstown is located on the shores of Otsego Lake.

The word *otsego* is a Native American name meaning "place of the rock." Visitors can still see the rock, called Council Rock, in the lake today. James Fenimore Cooper called the lake Glimmerglass in his books. On the eastern shore of the lake, there's a small castle that was built just to be pretty. It's only accessible from the lake, but no visitors are allowed.

✬ Mike's All-Star ✬ Blue Chip Muffins

Makes 12 muffins

Here's a recipe for the Blue Chip Muffins that Kate and I had for breakfast at the Hall of Fame. They are my favorite muffins because they're chocolate and blueberry! That's like a walk-off home run! I make them with my mom. (Don't tell her, but sometimes I try to sneak extra chocolate chips into the batter!) Now you can make them, too (with an adult's help). —Mike

Ingredients

2 cups all-purpose flour
1/2 cup granulated sugar
1/4 teaspoon salt
2 teaspoons baking powder
1/4 teaspoon cinnamon
2 eggs
1 cup milk
1/4 cup (1/2 stick) melted butter, slightly cooled

1 teaspoon vanilla extract
1/2 cup chocolate chips
1 cup frozen wild blueberries (do not defrost)
   or fresh blueberries
Optional: sanding sugar to sprinkle on top

Directions

Preheat oven to 375 degrees Fahrenheit. Place baking cups in a muffin pan.

In a large bowl, mix together flour, sugar, salt, baking powder, and cinnamon. Add eggs, milk, melted butter, and vanilla. Mix the ingredients just until they are combined. Do not overmix.

Stir in chocolate chips. Using a spatula, gently fold in blueberries. Be careful not to crush the berries.

Spoon batter into the prepared pan. Baking cups will be nearly full. Top each muffin with a sprinkle of sanding sugar, if desired.

Bake 23–27 minutes, or until golden brown.

Looking for more sports stories?

Read on for a peek at the first book
in David A. Kelly's MVP series.

CHECK THE BLUEPRINTS

The side door of the school flew open, and Max and Alice ran out. "They can't cancel the Olympics!" Max said. "We've got to tell the others."

Alice pointed to a big grassy field next to the school. "There they are," she said.

On the field, an oval racetrack had been marked out with wooden sticks and a rope. Luke and Kat were standing at the starting line that had been drawn on the grass with white chalk. Next to them was Nico, a tall boy with straight dark hair. He was one of Franklin's best athletes. Ms. Suraci, the school's PE teacher, stood nearby. She had a ponytail and wore a blue tracksuit with stripes on the side.

Max and Alice began to run over, but before they reached the starting line, Ms. Suraci held out her phone with the speaker on. They heard a voice say *"Three, two, one, go!"* and a loud buzzer split the air. The race had started! Luke, Nico, and Kat took off running. Kat quickly took the lead, with Nico hot on her heels.

Max and Alice stopped to cheer them on.

"Come on, Kat!" Alice yelled.

"Go, Nico!" Max shouted.

As the three rounded the far end of the racecourse, Nico pulled ahead of Kat. Kat's curly hair bounced up and down as she tried to catch up with him.

But Nico's long, tall body had an advantage. He was pumping his arms and running as fast as he could.

Max and Alice cheered them as they rounded the final corner. Ms. Suraci was standing at the finish line. Nico flew across the line first! Then Kat zoomed across. The bright purple ribbons holding back her curly hair streamed along behind her.

Luke finished last. He was panting and out of breath.

"Nico wins the gold!" Ms. Suraci called out. "Kat gets silver! And Luke wins bronze!"

Kat and Luke flopped on the ground to catch their breath, but Nico punched his fist into the air. "Yeah!" he said. "A gold medal in running would be great, but I really want to win the gold in gymnastics."

"No one else has a chance," Alice

said. "You're our top tumbler!" She gave Nico a high five.

As the clap from the high five echoed in the air, Nico dropped his hands to the ground and flipped his feet up over his head. His body arched into a circle as he turned two perfect handsprings!

Nico landed right in front of Max. "Ta-da!" he said. Nico loved to show off. His long arms and legs made him good at running, jumping, twisting, bouncing, flipping, spinning, and anything else that would make most other people queasy.

Alice and Ms. Suraci clapped. Then Ms. Suraci pretended to put medals around each of the runners' necks, just like they did at the real Olympics. When she was finished, Ms. Suraci checked her watch. "That was fun, kids," she said. "But I have to get going. I'll be rooting for you at the big race tomorrow!"

The kids waved goodbye to Ms. Suraci. She walked across the field to the teachers' parking lot behind the school. When she was safely out of earshot, Max leaned over to the group.

"Make sure you enjoy those medals," Max said. "Because you might not have a chance to win one tomorrow!"

Everyone looked at Max. "What do you mean?" Nico asked.

"We just heard the Olympics might be canceled!" Alice answered.

"Why?" Kat asked.

"Someone has been sending threatening messages to the school," Alice said. "We found a note saying the school should call off the Olympics."

"They can't do that!" Nico said. He slumped to the grass.

"Maybe we can figure out who did it," Kat said. "We should look for clues."

"That's what I was thinking. We need

to find out who's making our Olympics a mess!" Max said. "And I know where to start!"

Max always had a plan. He reached into his back pocket and pulled out the envelope. He held it so they could read the BEWARE warning.

"Alice and I snagged this from the trash can in the main office," Max said. "It's the envelope the note came in. I was going to try to dust it for fingerprints, so just hold it by the edges."

Max passed the envelope to Kat. She took it gently by the corners and turned it over to look at each side.

"Um, Max?" Kat said. "I don't think you need to dust this envelope for fingerprints."

"What do you mean?" Max asked.

Kat pointed at the flap on the back of the envelope. There, right above the sticky part, were two bright blue fingerprints!

"It looks like you've already found the fingerprints of the person who's threatening the Olympics!" Kat said.

The kids huddled around Kat to get a better look. The fingerprints seemed like a deep blue smudge, unless you looked closely.

"Let me see that," Max said. He took the envelope back from Kat and studied the fingerprints. Close up, he could see small, ridged lines. Max took out his phone and snapped a picture of the fingerprint. He zoomed in on the photo. It was easy to see a big swirl and lots of wavy lines. He showed his friends.

"Wow! Good thinking, Max," Luke said.

"Look at that radial loop," Max said, pointing to the screen. "And that second finger has a clear arch. These are great clues!"

"What if they came from Mrs. Doolin when she opened the envelope?" Luke asked. "Maybe she had ink on her hands or something."

"Good idea, but I don't think so," Alice said. "This looks like paint."

Alice used her fingernail to scratch off a small part of one of the blue fingerprints. Tiny blue flakes rubbed off.

"It wouldn't rub off if it was ink," Alice said. "Whoever wrote this note must have been using paint."

"Exactly," Max said. "So all we have to do to catch the Olympic troublemaker is find a match for these fingerprints!"

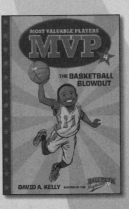

New friends. New adventures.
Find a new series ... just for you!

Illustrations (from left to right) : © Mark Meyers; © Mike Boldt; © Brigette Barrager; © Qin Leng; © Russ Cox; © Wesley Lowe

BALLPARK *Mysteries*
FOR THE SPORTS FAN

The DINO FILES
FOR THE ADVENTURER

Louise Trapeze
FOR THE SUPERSTAR

PIPER GREEN
FOR THE DREAMER

PUPPY PIRATES
FOR THE ANIMAL LOVER

Totally True adventures!
FOR THE EXPLORER

RandomHouseKids.com